HONK FINDS A MOON BEAM

Written by Richard Hays
Illustrated by Chris Sharp

D1451620

Faith Kids®
is an imprint of Cook Communications Ministries,
Colorado Springs, Colorado 80918
Cook Communications, Paris, Ontario
Kingsway Communications, Eastbourne, England

HONK FINDS A MOONBEAM
©2001 by The Illustrated Word, Inc.

First printing, 2001
Printed in Canada
05 04 03 02 01   5 4 3 2 1

Digital art and design: Gary Currant
Executive Producer: Kenneth R. Wilcox

Honk Finds a Moonbeam

Life Issue: My children need to learn to act responsibly.

Spiritual Building Block: Responsibility

Sound: Next time you are in the car together, tell your children you have a new traveling game. For every activity you name off, your children have to come up with a more responsible activity. For example: "I immediately followed the ball into the street when it rolled past me," could be followed by "I checked if any cars were coming before I went to get the ball"; or, "I touched the stove to see if it was still hot," could be followed by "I stayed away from the stove in case it was still hot."

Sight: With a kind and helpful attitude, help your children clean and organize their bedrooms. When you are finished, have your kids grab the camera and take a picture of the room in this excellent state. Hang the photos in prominent places in the bedrooms to remind your kids of how their rooms can look.

Touch: For each time your children start their homework without your reminder or clean their bedrooms before coming down for breakfast Saturday morning or pack up their lunches for school without being told, reward them with extra minutes of computer time or a special snack or a small gift—and lots of praise.

Honk the camel looked up from his workbench where he was building his latest invention.

A huge full moon was rising over Noah's Park. It was the largest moon Honk had ever seen.

"That's amazing," Honk whispered to himself. "Wouldn't it be wonderful to walk on the moon? It must be so clean up there."

"Honk, we don't need another camel on the moon," laughed Screech the monkey as he scampered into the clearing. "There's already a camel up there! Look!"

Honk looked up and stared at the moon. He gasped. Screech was right. It did look like there was a camel on the moon. It had two humps and four legs and a fine-looking face. You are a very handsome camel, but how did you get on the moon? wondered Honk.

"Honk! Honk!" called out Stretch the giraffe.

"I'm over here, Stretch," Honk said as he continued staring up at the moon.

Stretch limped up to Honk's workbench. She was bent over and wore a large bandage on her neck. She was in pain!

"What's wrong, Stretch?" asked Honk, now concerned about his friend.

"My neck is so stiff I can hardly lift up my head. Now I can't reach the treetops where the tender leaves are. Can you make something that will lift me to the top of the trees until my neck heals? This is the worst thing that could ever happen to a giraffe.

"Of course, Stretch," Honk agreed, looking up at the moon again. "At least I can try."

Wispy clouds drifted into the sky, partially covering the moon. Honk began to work on something to help Stretch. Within a few hours he took a strange-looking device over to Stretch's favorite tall tree. The grateful giraffe followed.

"Will this work, Honk?" Stretch asked doubtfully.

"I think so," Honk said. He tossed a vine over the highest limb he could reach and threaded it through his invention.

"When I pull on this vine, it will lift you into the tree where you can eat all the leaves you want."

Honk pulled on the vine, and Stretch rose into the tree. Honk glanced up. The moon was again shining brightly through a hole in the clouds. He stared at the moon and kept pulling.

"Honk," said Stretch, "I don't think this is working. The vine is slipping! It doesn't feel good. Honk, are you listening?"

Unfortunately, Honk was not listening. The camel was moonstruck.

Stretch began to panic.

"Help! Someone, help!" yelled Stretch. She was hanging from the tree while Honk just stared at the moon and pulled on the vine!

Howler the lion and Ponder the frog were talking near Polka Dot Pond when they heard Stretch's cry for help. Howler scooped up the little frog and raced over to the tree where Stretch was hanging.

Ponder yelled at Honk, "Stop pulling on the vine, Honk!" Howler leaped up and sliced through the vine with his claws. Stretch dropped to the ground with a thud. "Ouch!" she shrieked. "Stretch, are you all right?" Ponder asked. A gust of wind whipped through the park, knocking Ponder off his feet. Ponder hopped up, but now the wind began to blow harder and a torrential rain poured down on Noah's Park.

"It's a storm," yelled Ponder. "Take shelter in Cozy Cave!"

As the last animal reached the safety of the cave, a bolt of lightning struck a rock above the opening. A piece of the rock shaped like half a moon broke off and fell to the ground.

The storm menaced the park for a week. Most of the animals slept and played in the cave. Only Honk stared at the stormy sky, thinking about the unseen moon.

When the storm finally stopped, the animals ran happily out into a cool, clear evening. Screech was the last one out of the cave, but as he rushed to join the others, he tripped over a rock. What's this? he wondered. He picked up the rock and yelped when he saw the half-moon shape.

"Honk! Honk!" Screech yelled. "Come over here. I found a piece of the moon. It must have fallen from the sky."

Honk ran over and grabbed the rock from Screech. He looked up at the half moon in the sky and at the rock. "It does look like a piece of the moon. What should we do? What should we do?"

"That's not a piece of the moon, Honk," Ponder laughed gently. "The moon is high in the sky. How could a piece of the moon end up in Noah's Park?"

"It is a piece of the moon, Ponder," said Honk. "See? It's the same shape as the moon. It's like a... a moonbeam, and I must put it back where it belongs!"

Honk sat at his workbench and shook his head. He really had no idea how to put the moonbeam back in the sky. It seemed that only God could do such a thing. Maybe God could use some help, though. Honk smiled and began to work.

Using a stick dipped in berry juice, Honk sketched out a couple of ideas on a piece of tree bark. He decided the first idea might work.

Honk found a forked tree branch and a short piece of vine. He soaked the vine with rubbery sap until it stretched. Then he tied the ends to the branch. Perfect! he thought. I'll call it a flinger, he decided.

Honk found a small stone, placed it in the flinger, and stretched the vine back as far as he could. He let go. The stone flew across the pond. The flinger worked!

The next day Honk built a much bigger flinger. This one stretched between two trees. He needed this giant flinger to put the moonbeam back in the sky.

Across the pond, the other animals watched Honk.

"Too bad he doesn't spend the time making something to help Stretch," said Shadow.

"Yes, instead of wasting time on hurling a rock into space," agreed Screech, sheepishly, "even if I did find the rock."

"Honk believes that this is his responsibility. He is trying to do the right thing," Ponder reminded them. "Being responsible is very important."

Meanwhile, Honk, who was testing the big flinger, sailed across the pond and landed in a heap in front of his friends.

"Maybe I should let go of the rock first," Honk snickered.

Honk spent the next few days at his drawing board working on another idea. The flinger was too dangerous! Stretch came by to ask if Honk had made something to help her reach tender leaves at the top of the trees.

"My neck is still very sore," explained Stretch.

"I do have an idea that might help you," said Honk, "but first I must get the moonbeam back to the moon."

When Stretch left, Honk began to work on what he called a sky climber. He laid two long sticks on the ground and tied shorter sticks between them. Then he added more sticks to make the climber longer.

When he leaned it against Stretch's favorite tree to see how high it would go, he realized that this idea would not work either. It was simply too far to the moon.

Honk slumped in front of Ponder.

"This isn't working," the dejected camel told the frog. "I don't know how to get the moonbeam back to the moon. I have failed."

"You haven't failed, Honk," Ponder smiled. "You have tried your hardest to be responsible. No one can ask more of you."

"But I have let God down." Honk shook his head.

"No you haven't. Moonbeams are something God takes care of, not us. But I think God is very proud of you for trying. I know I am," Ponder told the camel. "Now maybe you can help Stretch. You have a responsibility to your friends, too."

Across the pond Stretch found the sky climber Honk had left leaning against her favorite tree. This must be the invention Honk promised to make, she thought. I'll just try it out. I am so hungry!

Stretch began to climb, but when she reached the top, she was still short of the juiciest leaves. She looked down and saw she could go up on more stick on the climber. She stepped on that very last stick and reached out. Her foot slipped and she began to sway back and forth on the very top of the climber! "Help!" she yelled.

Honk was taking the giant flinger apart when he glanced across the pond and saw Stretch climbing to the top of the big tree. Maybe I should call it a tree climber, thought Honk. Then he saw Stretch take the last step. "Don't step on the top stick, Stretch," Honk screamed. She was going to fall!

Honk acted quickly. He placed himself on the flinger and pushed the vine back as far as he could until it almost snapped. He carefully aimed himself at Stretch's tree and jumped up. The flinger launched him with a loud SPRONG!"

Honk sailed across the pond again. As he passed the tree, he grabbed Stretch just as she fell from the climber. They tumbled over and over until they landed with a splash in the pond.

The other animals cheered as they pulled Honk and Stretch out of the pond. Dreamer patted Honk on his back and Ivory hugged Stretch. Stretch lifted her neck and laughed with surprise, "It doesn't hurt anymore, Honk. When you grabbed me, you must have stretched it back into place. Now I can eat again! Oh, thans you, Honk." Stretch giggled. "Oh, and thanks for saving my life, too."

"It was nothing," said Honk bashfully. "I'm sorry I didn't help you before."

"That's okay, Honk." Stretch smiled. "I needed to lose a little weight anyway."

Later that night when the moon came out, it was once again full and bright. Honk and Ponder sat on the sand, tossing rocks into the pond.

Honk sighed. "Do you think anyone will ever go to the moon, Ponder?"

"I don't know, Honk," answered the wise frog. "God helped Noah build the ark to save all the animals. Maybe someday God will help someone else build a ship that will fly to the moon. It could be a camel, or maybe even a frog." Honk looked up at the moon. Now a frog in the moon looked back down at him. He and Ponder both laughed.

The End

DREAMER HAS A NIGHTMARE

Dreamer the rhinoceros loves to dream, until one day he has his first nightmare. How will Dreamer handle this frightening experience? Discover the answer in the Noah's Park adventure, Dreamer Has a Nightmare.

STRETCH'S TREASURE HUNT

Stretch the giraffe grew up watching her parents search for the Treasure of Nosy Rock. Imagine what happens when she finds out that the treasure might be buried in Noah's Park. Watch the fur fly as Stretch and her friends look for treasure in Stretch's Treasure Hunt.

CAMELS DON'T FLY

Honk the camel finds a statue of a camel with wings. Now, he is convinced that he can fly, too. Will Honk be the first camel to fly? Find out in the Noah's Park adventure, Camels Don't Fly.

HONK'S BIG ADVENTURE

On the first day of spring, all the animals of Noah's Park are playing in the mud, water, and leaves. This good clean fun creates a lot of dirty animals. When Honk the camel sees the mess, he decides to leave Noah's Park and find a clean place to live. Will Honk find what he searches for? Find out in the hilarious Noah's Park story, Honk's Big Adventure.

PONDER MEETS THE POLKA DOTS

Ponder the frog is growing lily pads in the Noah's Park pond. When something starts eating the lily pads, the normally calm frog decides to get even. Will Ponder save his lily pads? Find out in the colorful Noah's Park adventure, Ponder Meets the Polka Dots.